Little Women

Little Women

LOUISA MAY ALCOTT

Condensed and adapted by
Bethany Snyder

Illustrated by
Martin Hargreaves

Cover illustrated by
Bill Maughan

Plate colorization by
Jerry Dillingham

Dalmatian Press

The Dalmatian Press Great Classics for Children
have been adapted and illustrated with care and thought,
to introduce you to a world of famous authors, characters, ideas,
and stories that have been loved for generations.

Editor — Kathryn Knight
Creative Director — Gina Rhodes
And the entire classics project team of Dalmatian Press

All art and adapted text © Dalmatian Press, LLC

ISBN: 1-40370-596-8

First Published in the United States in 2003 by Dalmatian Press, LLC, USA

Copyright © 2003 Dalmatian Press, LLC

Printed and bound in China.

The DALMATIAN PRESS name and logo are
trademarks of Dalmatian Press, LLC, Franklin, Tennessee 37067.

12899

04 05 06 07 15 14 13 12 11 10 9 8 7 6 5 4 3 2

A note to the reader—

A classic story rests in your hands. The characters are famous. The tale is timeless.

This Great Classic for Children by Dalmatian Press has been carefully condensed and adapted from the original version (which you really *must* read when you're ready for every detail). We kept the well-known phrases for you. We kept the author's style. And we kept the important imagery and heart of the tale.

Literature is terrific fun! It encourages you to think. It helps you dream. It is full of heroes and villains, suspense and humor, adventure and wonder, and new ideas. It introduces you to writers who reach out across time to say: "Do you want to hear a story I wrote?"

Curl up and enjoy.

DALMATIAN PRESS
GREAT CLASSICS FOR CHILDREN

CONTENTS

CHARACTERS

THE March Family

MEG — (Margaret) 16, very pretty and sensible—with dreams of living in fine style

JO — (Josephine) 15, very tall, thin, and headstrong—with a talent for writing

BETH — (Elizabeth) 13, sweet, caring, and musically talented—but timid and shy

AMY — 12, a bit selfish, though well-mannered and ladylike—with artistic talents

MARMEE — Mrs. March, a helpful, cheery woman—the most splendid mother in the world

FATHER — Mr. March, who is off at war, serving as a chaplain

HANNAH — the family housekeeper

THE HUMMELS — a poor family with a sick newborn baby

THE KINGS — the family that Meg works for as a governess

CHARACTERS

AUNT MARCH — the grumpy old great-aunt who employs Jo to keep her company

LAURIE LAURENCE — 16, the spirited boy who lives next door to the Marches

MR. LAURENCE — Laurie's grandfather, the old gentleman next door

MR. JOHN BROOKE — Laurie's tutor, who casts his handsome brown eyes on Meg

ANNIE, BELLE, AND NED MOFFAT — Meg's friends

SALLIE GARDINER — Meg's friend

KATE, FRED, FRANK, AND GRACE — Laurie's friends from England

CHAPTER ONE

Marmee's Girls

"Christmas won't be Christmas without any presents," grumbled Jo, lying on the rug.

"It's so dreadful to be poor!" sighed Meg, looking down at her old dress.

"It's not fair. Some girls have plenty of pretty things, and others have nothing at all," added little Amy with a sniff.

"We've got Father and Mother, and each other," said Beth happily from her corner.

The four young faces brightened in the firelight. Then Jo said sadly, "We *haven't* got Father, and won't for a long time." The four were silent, thinking of Father far away where the fighting was.

They missed him, but they were proud of their father. He was too old to be a soldier, but he was serving as a chaplain in the war between the states.

Meg said, "Mother thinks we shouldn't spend money on Christmas presents when our men are suffering in the army. But I am afraid I don't like the idea." Meg shook her head as she thought of all the pretty things she wanted.

"We only have a dollar each to spend," said Jo. "Surely the army won't miss that. I so wanted to buy a new book."

"I planned to spend mine on new sheet music," said Beth with a little sigh.

"I shall get a box of drawing pencils," said Amy.

"Let's each buy what we want, and have a little fun. We work hard enough to earn it," cried Jo.

"I know *I* do—teaching those King children nearly all day," complained Meg.

"How would you like to care for a grumpy old lady like Aunt March all the time?" asked Jo.

"I think washing dishes and keeping things tidy is the worst work in the world." Beth looked at her rough hands with a sigh.

"At least you don't have to go to school with rude girls who laugh at your dresses," cried Amy.

"Don't you wish we had the money Papa lost when we were little, Jo?" asked Meg, who could remember better times.

"You said the other day you thought we were happier than the King children. You said they fight all the time, in spite of their money," said Beth.

"So I did, Beth. Even though we *do* have to work, we are a pretty jolly set."

Jo got up from the rug, put her hands in her pockets, and began to whistle.

"Don't, Jo. It's so boyish," said Amy.

"You should remember that you are a young lady, Jo," added Meg. "Now that you are fifteen and you wear your hair up…"

"If putting up my hair makes me a lady, I'll wear it in two tails till I'm twenty," cried Jo. "I hate to think I've got to grow up, and wear long gowns, and look nice!"

"As for you, Amy," continued Meg, "you are too critical. You'll grow up a snobby little goose, if you don't take care."

"If Jo is a tomboy and Amy a goose, what am I, please?" asked Beth.

"You're a dear," answered Meg warmly. No one disagreed, for Beth was the pet of the family.

For you, dear reader, we will take this moment to give a little sketch of the four sisters.

Margaret, the oldest, was sixteen, and very pretty. She was plump and fair, with large eyes, soft brown hair, a sweet mouth, and white hands, of which she was rather proud.

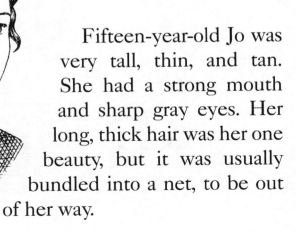

Fifteen-year-old Jo was very tall, thin, and tan. She had a strong mouth and sharp gray eyes. Her long, thick hair was her one beauty, but it was usually bundled into a net, to be out of her way.

Beth was a rosy, bright-eyed girl of thirteen. She had a shy manner, a soft voice, and a peaceful expression. She seemed to live in a happy world of her own, only going out to meet the few people whom she trusted and loved.

Amy, the youngest, was a most important person— in her own opinion at least. She had blue eyes and curling yellow hair. She was pale and slender, and was always mindful of her manners.

The clock struck six. Beth put a pair of slippers down to warm by the fire. Mother was coming, and everyone brightened to welcome her. Meg lit the lamp, and Amy got out of the easy chair without being asked. Jo held the slippers closer to the fire and said, "These are quite worn out. Marmee should have a new pair."

"I know!" said Beth. "Let's each get Marmee a Christmas gift, and not get anything for ourselves."

Meg looked at her own pretty hands. "I shall give her a nice pair of gloves."

"Army shoes," cried Jo.

"Some handkerchiefs," said Beth.

"I'll get a little bottle of perfume. I may even have some left to buy my pencils," added Amy.

"Let Marmee *think* we are getting things for ourselves, and then surprise her," said Jo. "We'll do our secret shopping tomorrow afternoon."

All four girls hooted with delight at the idea.

"Glad to find you so merry, my girls," said a cheery voice at the door. They all turned to welcome a tall, motherly lady. She was not elegantly dressed, but the girls thought the gray cloak and simple bonnet covered the most splendid mother in the world.

Mrs. March got her wet things off and her warm slippers on. Sitting down in the easy chair, she drew Amy to her lap. Meg arranged the tea table, and Jo brought wood and set chairs. Beth trotted between the parlor and the kitchen, while Amy gave directions to everyone.

After dinner, Mrs. March said, "I've got a treat for you. It's a nice long letter from Father. He sends loving wishes for Christmas, and a special message to you girls." She patted her pocket as if she had a treasure there.

"When will he come home, Marmee?" asked Beth with a little quiver in her voice.

"Not for many months, dear. He will stay as long as he can. Now come and hear the letter."

It was a cheerful, hopeful letter, full of lively descriptions of camp life, marches, and military news. At the end, Father sent a special message to his little girls at home.

"Give them all of my love and a kiss. Tell them I think of them by day and pray for them by night. I know they will be loving children to you, and do their duty faithfully. And when I come back to them I may be prouder than ever of my little women."

Everybody sniffed at that part. Amy hid her face on her mother's shoulder and sobbed, "I *am* a selfish girl! But I'll truly try to be better."

"We all will!" cried Meg. "I think too much of my looks and hate to work, but won't any more, if I can help it."

"I'll try not to be rough and wild. I'll do my duty here instead of wanting to be somewhere else," said Jo.

Beth said nothing. She wiped away her tears and began to knit a blue army sock with all her might. She resolved in her quiet little soul to be all that Father hoped for when he came home.

Mrs. March said, "We have many burdens on our road to happiness. Our longing for goodness and happiness helps us through troubles and mistakes. Now, my dears, suppose you see how far on the road to goodness and happiness you can get before Father comes home."

"What are our burdens, Mother?" asked Amy.

"Each of you told what your burden was just now, except Beth," said her mother.

Shy, quiet Beth said, "Mine is dishes and dusting, and envying girls with nice pianos, and being afraid of people."

"Let us do it," said Meg. "It is only another name for trying to be good. We *want* to be good, but it's hard work and we forget."

"I will always be here to guide you," said their warm, thoughtful mother.

Hannah, their housekeeper, cleared the table. Then the girls worked on their sewing jobs. At nine they stopped work and sang, as usual, before they went to bed. No one but Beth could get much music out of the old piano, but she had a way of softly touching the yellowed keys. It had become a household custom to sing in the evening, for Mother was a born singer. Her cheerful singing was the first and last sound the girls heard every day.

CHAPTER TWO

Merry Christmas

Jo was the first to wake in the gray dawn of Christmas morning. No stockings hung at the fireplace in their room, and for a moment she felt disappointed. Then winter sunshine crept in to touch the bright heads of her sisters with a Christmas greeting. Soon, all the girls were up and running downstairs with a basket of secret gifts.

"Where is Mother, Hannah?" asked Meg.

"Goodness only knows," said the housekeeper. "Some poor creature came a-beggin', and your ma went to see what was needed."

"She will be back soon, so have everything ready," said Meg, looking over the presents.

"My handkerchiefs look nice, don't they?" said Beth, looking proudly at her work.

A door slammed and steps sounded in the hall.

"There's Mother. Hide the basket!" cried Jo.

The basket of gifts went under the sofa. The girls went to the table, eager for breakfast.

"Merry Christmas, Marmee!" they all cried.

"Merry Christmas, little daughters! I'm glad to see you're ready for breakfast, but I have one word to say before we sit down. Not far from here lies a poor woman with a newborn baby. Six children huddle in one bed, for there is no fire. And they have nothing to eat. My girls, will you give the Hummels your breakfast as a Christmas present?"

The girls were all very hungry, and for a minute no one spoke. Then Jo exclaimed, "I'm so glad you came before we began!"

"May I help carry the things to the poor children?" asked Beth.

"*I* shall take the cream and the muffins," added Amy, giving up what she liked most.

Meg was already covering the pancakes.

"I thought you'd do it," said Mrs. March, smiling. "When we come back we will have bread and milk for breakfast, and make it up at dinner."

They arrived at a room with broken windows, no fire, a sick mother, and a group of pale children cuddled under one old quilt, trying to keep warm.

"It is good angels come to us!" said the woman, crying for joy.

"Funny angels in hoods and mittens," said Jo, and everyone laughed.

Hannah made a fire, and stuffed her own cloak into the broken windowpanes. Mrs. March gave the mother tea and broth. She dressed the little baby as tenderly as if it had been her own. The girls set the table, and fed the children like hungry birds.

That was a very happy breakfast, though the March ladies didn't get any of it. When they left the Hummels, the hungry little girls who gave away their breakfasts on Christmas morning were the merriest people in the city.

"That's loving our neighbor. I like it," said Meg, as they set out their presents while their mother was upstairs collecting clothes for the Hummels.

"She's coming! Play the piano, Beth! Open the door, Amy! Three cheers for Marmee!" cried Jo.

Their mother walked into the room and Meg led her to the seat of honor. Mrs. March was both surprised and touched by each of her presents. The slippers went on at once. A new handkerchief was slipped into her pocket, well scented with Amy's perfume. The nice gloves were a perfect fit.

Later that evening Hannah called the girls for supper. When they saw the table, they were amazed. There was ice cream and cake and fruit and four bouquets of flowers!

"Old Mr. Laurence from the big house next door sent all this," explained Mrs. March.

"The Laurence boy's grandfather? But we don't know him!" exclaimed Meg.

"Hannah told one of his servants about your breakfast party. It pleased him. He knew my father years ago," said their mother. "This afternoon he sent me a note to say how kind all of you were. So now you have a little feast at night to make up for the bread-and-milk breakfast."

"His grandson put it into his head, I know he did! I wish we could get to know him. But he's so shy," said Jo, as the plates went round. "Our cat ran away once, and he brought her back. He needs fun, I'm sure he does," she added.

"I like the boy's manners," said Marmee. "He brought the flowers himself, and I should have asked him in. He looked so sad as he went away. He seemed to have no fun of his own."

Beth nestled up to her. She whispered softly, "I wish I could send my fun to Father. I'm afraid he isn't having such a merry Christmas."

*"I know," said Beth. "Let's each get Marmee
a Christmas gift, and not get anything for ourselves."*

She was not elegantly dressed, but the girls thought the gray cloak and simple bonnet covered the most splendid mother in the world.

She was surprised to find herself face to face
with the "Laurence boy."

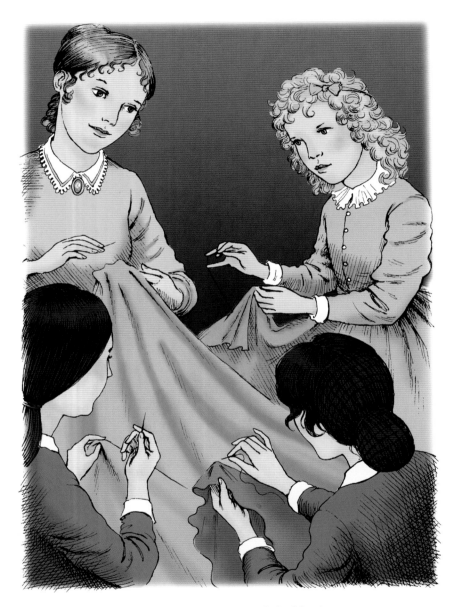

*They promised to enjoy their blessings
and try to deserve them.*

CHAPTER THREE

The Laurence Boy

"Jo! Jo! We have an invitation for tomorrow night!" cried Meg. She found Jo reading and eating apples in her favorite window seat with her pet rat. She read the note to Jo. " 'Mrs. Gardiner would be happy to see Miss Margaret and Miss Josephine at a dance on New Year's Eve.' What shall we wear?"

"You know we each only have one nice dress for parties," answered Jo. "Yours is as good as new, but I have a burn in the back of mine. What shall *I* do?"

"Sit still and keep your back out of sight. The front is all right," replied Meg.

On New Year's Eve there was a great deal of running up and down, and laughing and talking.

After a few mishaps, Meg was finished at last. With help from the entire family, Jo's hair was arranged and her dress put on. Meg's high-heeled shoes were very tight, though she would not admit it. Jo's nineteen hairpins all seemed stuck into her head.

The girls seldom went to parties, and so they were quite nervous as they walked down the road with Hannah. But Mrs. Gardiner greeted them kindly. Meg knew her daughter, Sallie, and was at her ease very soon. But Jo felt as much out of place as a colt in a flower garden.

Jo decided to hide behind a curtain in a hallway. When she ducked in, she was surprised to find herself face to face with the "Laurence boy."

"Dear me, I didn't know anyone was here!" stammered Jo. "Did I disturb you?"

"Not a bit. I only came here because I don't know many people and felt rather strange."

"So did I." The boy sat down and looked at his shoes, till Jo said, "You live near us, don't you?"

The boy laughed, "Only next door. How is your little run-away cat doing, Miss March?" His black eyes shone with fun.

"Nicely, thank you, Mr. Laurence," said Jo with a smile. "And thank you for the food at Christmas."

"Grandpa sent it, Miss March."

"But *you* gave him the idea. And I'm not Miss March—I'm only Jo."

"And I'm only Laurie. Do you like to dance, Miss Jo?" he asked.

"I do if there is plenty of room, and everyone is lively. In a place like this I'm sure to step on people's toes. I keep out of mischief and let Meg dance. Do you dance?"

"Sometimes. I've been in Europe a good many years, and haven't been out in company enough yet to know how you do things here."

They chatted until they felt like old friends. Jo took several good looks at Laurie. She wanted to be able to describe him to her sisters. She said to herself, "Curly black hair, brown skin, big black eyes. Handsome nose, fine teeth, small hands and feet. Taller than I am. Very polite, for a boy, and altogether jolly."

"I suppose you are going to college soon?" she asked him.

Laurie shrugged. "Not for a year or two."

"Are you but fifteen?" asked Jo, looking at the tall lad.

"Sixteen, next month."

"How I wish *I* was going to college! You don't look as if you like the idea."

"I hate it!"

"What *do* you like?"

"To live in Italy, and to enjoy myself in my own way."

Jo wanted very much to ask what his own way was, but his black eyebrows and serious look made her change the subject. "That's a splendid polka! Why don't you go and try it?"

"If you will come, too," he answered with a polite little bow. "There's a long hall out there, and we can dance grandly, and no one will see us. Please come."

Jo thanked him and gladly went. They had a grand polka, for Laurie danced well.

When it was time to leave, Jo found that Meg had sprained her ankle dancing in her high-heeled shoes. It was too painful to walk on all the way home—and it had started to rain. Laurie offered the use of his grandfather's carriage, which had just pulled up outside.

Laurie sat up top with the driver while Jo, Meg, and Hannah rode below. The ladies rolled away inside the carriage, feeling very festive and elegant.

"I had a wonderful time. Did you?" asked Jo. She rumpled up her hair, making herself comfortable.

"Yes, till I hurt myself," answered Meg. "What were you doing, hidden away there?"

Jo told her about her talk and her polka with the Laurence boy. By the time she had finished, they were home.

With many thanks, they said good-night to Laurie. They were hoping not to disturb anyone, but the instant their door creaked, two sleepy voices cried out:

"Tell about the party! Tell about the party!"

CHAPTER FOUR

Burdens and Blessings

"Oh, dear. It is so hard to go back to our duties," sighed Meg the morning after the party.

The holidays were now over.

"I wish it was Christmas or New Year's all the time. Wouldn't it be fun?" answered Jo, yawning.

"We wouldn't enjoy ourselves half so much. But it does seem so nice to go to parties and read and rest and not work," said Meg.

Everyone seemed rather out of sorts that morning. Beth had a headache and lay on the sofa, trying to comfort herself with the cat and three kittens. Amy was fretting because she hadn't learned her school lessons, and she couldn't find her boots. Jo whistled and made a great racket getting ready. Mrs. March was very busy trying to finish a letter, and Hannah had the grumps.

"There never was such a cross family!" cried Jo. She had just upset an inkstand, broken both boot strings, and sat down upon her hat.

"You're the crossest person in it!" said Amy.

"Girls, girls, do be quiet one minute!" cried Mrs. March.

"Good-bye, Marmee," called out Jo. "We may be rascals this morning, but we'll come home angels tonight! Come on, Meg."

Jo and Meg left together for their jobs. Jo went off to tend old Aunt March and Meg to be governess to the King children. They looked back at the corner, for their mother was always at the window, waving.

Meg had a small salary as a governess. She tried not to be envious, but she *did* wish for pretty things and a happy life. At the Kings' she saw the older sisters' dainty ball dresses and bouquets. She heard lively gossip about theaters, concerts, sleighing, and parties. Meg did not complain much, but she was often bitter. She had not yet learned to know how rich she was in the blessings of home and family.

Jo happened to suit old Aunt March, who was lame and needed an active person to wait upon her. This did not suit Jo at all. But she got on very well thanks to a large library of fine books at Aunt March's house. Jo's greatest regret was that she couldn't read, run, and ride as much as she liked. A quick temper, sharp tongue, and restless spirit were always getting her into scrapes.

Beth was too bashful to go to school. She had tried, but suffered so much that it was given up. She did her lessons at home. She helped Hannah keep the home neat and comfortable. She was not lonely, for her world was filled with dolls, and she was by nature a busy bee. But she had her troubles as well. She longed very much to take music lessons and have a fine piano.

If anybody had asked Amy to name her greatest trial, she would have answered at once, "My nose." It was rather flat. Amy wanted a classic, straight nose, and drew whole sheets of handsome ones. She had a talent for drawing. She could also play twelve tunes, crochet, and read French without saying more than half of the words wrong. But things were seldom nice enough to please Amy. She was on her way to being a very spoiled little girl.

The two older girls took the younger sisters under their wings. Meg was Amy's closest friend, and Jo was gentle Beth's.

As the girls sat sewing that evening, Meg said, "Has anybody got anything to tell? It's been such a dismal day. I'm really dying for some amusement."

"I had a hard time with Aunt today," began Jo. "She is always so serious, and never lets herself have any fun. What a pleasant life she might have if only she chose! I don't envy her much, in spite of her money."

Meg said, "At the Kings' today I found everybody in a flurry. I was glad *I* didn't have any wild brothers to embarrass the family."

"I think being disgraced in school is a great deal *worser* than anything bad boys can do," said Amy. "Susie Perkins came to school today with a lovely red ring. I envied her so much. Till she got in trouble for drawing a picture of the teacher—and he took her by the ear—by the ear! Just imagine how horrid! I didn't envy her then."

Beth said, "I saw Mr. Laurence in the fish shop, but he didn't see me. He bought some fish for a poor woman who hadn't any dinner for her children. Wasn't it good of him?"

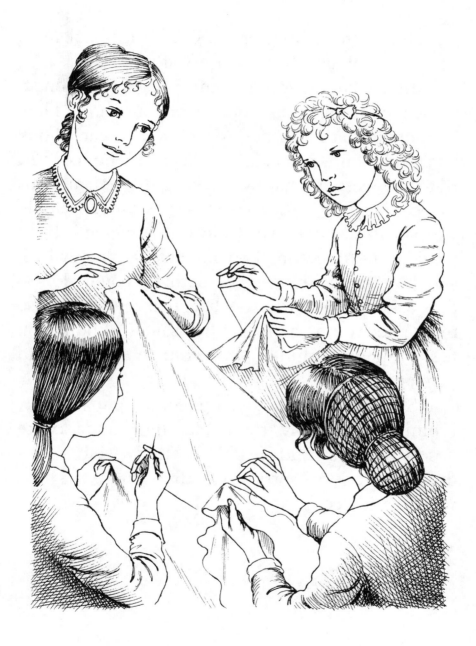

"Tell a story, Mother—one with a moral to it. I like to think about them afterward," said Jo.

Mrs. March smiled and began at once. "Once upon a time, there were four girls. They had enough to eat and drink and wear. They had kind friends and parents who loved them dearly. But they were not happy. These girls were anxious to be good, but were constantly saying, 'If only we had this,' or 'If we could only do that.' They were always forgetting how much they already had, and how many things they actually could do. So they asked an old woman what spell they could use to make them happy. She said, 'When you feel unhappy, think over your blessings, and be grateful.'

"So they agreed to stop complaining. They promised to enjoy their blessings and try to deserve them. And I believe they were never disappointed or sorry that they took the old woman's advice."

CHAPTER FIVE

Being Neighborly

A garden with a low hedge separated the Marches' house from that of Mr. Laurence. On one side was an old brown house. It was rather shabby without the vines and flowers that covered its walls in summer. On the other side was a stone mansion with a big coach house and neat lawns. Lovely things could be seen between the rich curtains.

Yet it seemed a lonely sort of house. No children played on the lawn. Few people went in and out. To Jo, this fine house next door seemed an enchanted palace. She had long wanted to see its glories and to know the Laurence boy. She had not seen him since the party.

"That boy needs to have fun," Jo said to herself as she walked by. "His grandpa does not know what's good for him, and keeps him shut up all alone to study."

She saw Mr. Laurence drive off. A curly black head was leaning on a thin hand at the upper window. "There he is," thought Jo. "Poor boy! All alone and looking sick this dismal day. I'll toss up a snowball and make him look out."

Up went a handful of soft snow, and the window opened at once. Jo laughed as she called out, "How do you do? Are you sick?"

Laurie leaned out and croaked, "Better, thank you. I've had a bad cold, and been shut up a week. It's dull up here."

"Isn't there some nice quiet girl who would amuse you?"

"Don't know any."

"You know us," laughed Jo. "I'm not quiet and nice, but I'll come."

Soon enough Jo appeared with a covered dish in one hand and Beth's three kittens in the other.

"What a cozy room this is," said Jo, looking around. "It only needs to have the hearth brushed and things straightened on the mantel. The books should be put here, and the pillows plumped up a bit. Now then, you're fixed." And so he was, for, as she laughed and talked, Jo had tidied the room.

"How kind you are!" Laurie said gratefully. "Now please let me do something to amuse you."

"No, I came to amuse *you*. Shall I read aloud?" and Jo looked toward some books nearby.

"Thank you, but I'd rather talk," said Laurie.

"I'll talk all day if you'll only set me going. Beth says I never know when to stop."

"Is Beth the rosy one who stays at home a good deal?" asked Laurie with interest.

"Yes, that's Beth."

"The pretty one is Meg, and the curly-haired one is Amy?"

"How did you find that out?"

Laurie blushed. "When I'm alone up here, I can't help looking over at your house. You always seem to be having such good times. It's like looking at a picture to see you all around the table with your mother. I haven't got any mother, you know." And Laurie poked the fire to hide a little twitching of the lips that he could not control.

The lonely look in his eyes went straight to Jo's warm heart. Laurie was sick and lonely. Feeling how rich she was in home and happiness, Jo gladly tried to share it with him.

"I wish you'd come over and see us," she said. "Mother would do you heaps of good, and Beth would sing to you, and Amy would dance. Meg and I would make you laugh, and we'd have jolly times. Wouldn't your grandpa let you?"

"I think he would, if your mother asked him. He's very kind, though he does not look so," Laurie said. "You see, Grandpa lives among his books. Mr. Brooke, my tutor, doesn't stay here. And I have no one to go around with, so I just stay home."

"You ought to go visiting. Then you'll have plenty of friends," said Jo.

Laurie offered to give Jo a tour of the house. He led the way from room to room until at last they came to the library. It was lined with books, and there were pictures and statues, and a great open fireplace.

"What richness!" sighed Jo, for she loved books. "Laurie, you ought to be the happiest boy in the world."

Laurie excused himself for a moment to see the doctor who had just arrived. Jo stood looking at a portrait of Mr. Laurence.

"I'm sure I wouldn't be afraid of him," she said out loud. "He's got kind eyes. He isn't as handsome as my grandfather, but I like him."

"Thank you, ma'am," said a gruff voice behind her. There, to her great dismay, stood old Mr. Laurence.

Poor Jo blushed, and her heart began to beat fast. The old gentleman said gruffly, "So you're not afraid of me, hey?"

"Not much, sir."

He gave a short laugh and shook her hand. "You've got your grandfather's spirit. He was a brave, honest man. I was proud to be his friend."

"Thank you, sir." And Jo was quite comfortable after that.

"What have you been doing to this boy of mine?" was the next question. "You think he needs cheering up a bit, do you?"

"Yes, sir, he seems a little lonely. Young folks would do him good. We are glad to help, for we don't forget the splendid Christmas present you sent us," said Jo.

Laurie returned, and Mr. Laurence noticed the change in his grandson as he talked and laughed with Jo. There was color, light, and life in the boy's face now. The girl was better than a doctor.

"She's right, the lad is lonely. I'll see what these little girls can do for him," thought Mr. Laurence.

They walked into the great drawing room. Jo noticed at once the grand piano.

"Do you play?" she asked, turning to Laurie. "I want to hear it, so I can tell Beth."

Laurie played and Jo listened. She wished Beth could hear him. She told Laurie how beautifully he played, and praised him so much that he blushed.

"That will do, young lady," interrupted the old man. "His music isn't bad, but I hope he will do as well in more important things. Going? I hope you'll come again. My respects to your mother. Good night, Doctor Jo." He shook hands kindly, but looked as if something did not please him.

When they got into the hall, Jo asked Laurie if she had said something wrong. He shook his head.

"No, it was me. He doesn't like to hear me play. Someday I'll tell you why. Thank you for coming."

"Well, take care, Laurie. Good night," said Jo.

"Good night, Jo, good night!"

When Jo had told her mother and sisters all about her visit with the neighbors, the family wished to go visiting at once. Mrs. March wanted to talk with the old gentleman because he had known her father. Meg longed to walk in the greenhouse. Beth sighed for the grand piano. Amy was eager to see the fine pictures and statues.

"Mother, why didn't Mr. Laurence like to have Laurie play the piano?" asked Jo.

"His son, Laurie's father, married an Italian lady. Mr. Laurence did not approve of her, even though she was a fine musician. He never saw his son after he married. They both died when Laurie was a little child. Laurie is like his mother and loves music. Perhaps his grandfather fears he may want to become a musician. At any rate, Laurie's skills must remind him of the woman he did not like."

"How silly!" said Jo. "Let him be a musician if he wants to."

CHAPTER SIX

Beth's Piano Lesson

The new friendship flourished like grass in spring. Everyone liked Laurie. And he told his tutor, Mr. Brooke, that "the Marches were splendid girls."

What good times they had—plays, sleigh rides, and skating parties. They had pleasant evenings in the Marches' old parlor, and little gatherings at the Laurences' great house. Meg walked in the greenhouse whenever she liked. Jo browsed over the new library. Amy copied pictures and enjoyed beauty to her heart's content.

Only Beth did not have the courage to visit. She went once with Jo, but the old gentleman stared at her so hard that she ran away.

But then Mr. Laurence mended matters. During one of his visits he started talking about Laurie's piano lessons and their grand piano. Beth found it impossible to stay in her distant corner. He said to Mrs. March, "Wouldn't some of your girls like to practice on the piano now and then, ma'am?"

Here he rose, as if to leave. A little hand slipped into his, and Beth looked up at him and said, "Oh, sir, they would—very, very much!"

"Are you the musical girl?" he asked. He looked down at her kindly.

"I'm Beth. I love music dearly. I'll come, if you are quite sure nobody will be disturbed."

"The house is empty half the day, so come as much as you like. I'll leave the side door open."

Beth gave the hand a grateful squeeze. The old gentleman kissed her cheek, saying softly, "I had a little girl once, with eyes like these. God bless you, my dear!" He went away in a great hurry.

Next day, Beth made her way like a mouse to the side door of the Laurences' house and into the drawing room. Quite by accident, of course, some easy music lay on the piano. With trembling fingers, Beth touched the keys. She immediately forgot everything but the happiness the music gave her.

After that, Beth played nearly every day. She never knew that Mr. Laurence opened his study door to hear the music. She never saw Laurie warn the servants away. She never suspected that the new music she found on the piano was put there for her. She simply enjoyed herself. And because she was so grateful for *this* blessing, a *greater* blessing was given to her.

Beth made Mr. Laurence some slippers as a thank-you gift. Several days passed after she and Laurie smuggled them into the study, but the old gentleman had said nothing about them. Then, one afternoon, Beth went out to do an errand. On her return, she saw four heads popping in and out of the parlor windows. Several hands waved, and joyful voices screamed.

"Here's a letter from the old gentleman! Come quick, and read it!"

At the door her sisters pulled her inside. Beth turned pale with delight and surprise. There stood a little piano, with a letter lying on the glossy lid.

"For me?" gasped Beth, holding onto Jo. "You read it! I can't. Oh, it is too lovely!"

Jo opened the paper and read:

Dear Madam—

I have had many pairs of slippers in my life, but never any I liked as much as yours. They will always remind me of you. I am sending you something which once belonged to the little granddaughter I lost. With hearty thanks and best wishes.

James Laurence

"You'll have to go and thank him," said Jo, but she was joking. She knew that shy Beth would never be able to face the old gentleman.

"Yes. I guess I'll go now, before I get frightened," Beth said. And then, to her family's surprise, she boldly walked next door to the Laurences' house.

They would have been still more amazed if they had seen what Beth did afterward. She knocked at the study door, went right up to Mr. Laurence, and held out her hand. Remembering that he had lost the little girl he loved, she put both arms round his neck and kissed his cheek.

Beth ceased to fear Mr. Laurence at that moment. She learned that love is more powerful than fear.

CHAPTER SEVEN

Amy Learns a Sour Lesson

"I hate being in debt," Amy said.

"In debt? What do you mean?" Meg asked.

Amy explained that the girls at school were giving out limes at recess. If one girl liked another girl, she gave her a lime. Amy had been given many, but hadn't any limes to share in return.

"How much money do you need?" asked Meg, taking out her purse.

"A quarter would more than do it." Meg handed her the money. "Oh, thank you! I'll have a grand feast, for I haven't tasted a lime this week."

Next day a rumor went round school that Amy March had twenty-four delicious limes and was going to treat her friends. Amy became quite the show-off as she displayed her great wealth of limes.

Jenny Snow was a young lady who had picked on Amy for not having limes before. *Now* she wanted to be friends again. But Amy had not forgotten the way Jenny had treated her. She said, "You needn't be so polite all of a sudden. You won't get any limes from me."

This made Jenny very angry. She quickly informed Mr. Davis, the teacher, that Amy had limes in her desk.

Now Mr. Davis had announced that no limes were to be in the classroom. He had promised to use his ruler on the first person to break the rules.

"Miss March, come here. Bring with you the limes you have in your desk."

Amy took out the limes and laid them before Mr. Davis.

"Now take these disgusting things and throw them out of the window."

Amy was red with shame and anger. She went to and fro six dreadful times. As she returned from her last trip, Mr. Davis said, "I am sorry this has happened, but I never allow my rules to be broken. Miss March, hold out your hand."

Too proud to cry or beg, Amy threw back her head bravely. She did not flinch as several tingling blows landed on her little palm. They did not hurt, but that made no difference. For the first time in her life, she had been struck. The disgrace was as deep as if he had knocked her down.

"You will now stand on the platform till recess," said Mr. Davis.

During the fifteen minutes that followed, the proud and sensitive little girl suffered a shame and pain which she never forgot. During the twelve years of her life she had been governed by love alone. Though both her hand and her heart ached, it was more painful to think of home. She thought, "They will be so disappointed in me!"

She was in a sad state when she got home. Her family did their best to comfort her, but Amy insisted that she would never return to school.

"Well, you can have a vacation. But I want you to study a little every day with Beth," said Mrs. March.

"That's good! It's terrible to think of those lovely limes," sighed Amy.

"I am not sorry you lost them. You broke the rules, and deserved some punishment," said Mrs. March. "But I do not agree with Mr. Davis's method."

"Are you glad I was disgraced before the whole school?" cried Amy.

"You are getting to be rather conceited, my dear. It's time you tried to correct it," replied her mother. "You have a good many little gifts. But there is no need of showing them off."

Amy was quiet for a moment. Then she asked, "Is Laurie a talented boy?"

"Yes. He has had an excellent education. And he has much talent," replied her mother.

"And he isn't stuck-up, is he?" asked Amy.

"Not in the least. That is why he is so charming and we all like him so much."

"I see. It's nice to have talents and be elegant. But it's not nice to show off," said Amy thoughtfully.

"Any more than it's proper to wear all your bonnets and gowns and ribbons at once—just so folks may know you've got them," added Jo. And the lesson ended in a laugh.

CHAPTER EIGHT

Jo Finds Some Weak Spots

"Tell me where you are going!" cried Amy one Saturday afternoon. Meg and Jo were getting ready to go out. "You might let *me* go. I haven't got anything to do."

"I can't, dear, because you aren't invited..." began Meg.

But Jo broke in impatiently, "You *can't* go, Amy. So don't be a baby and whine about it."

"You are going somewhere with Laurie, aren't you? Are you going to see a play at the theater?"

"Yes, we are. Now stop bothering us," said Jo.

"Please let me go," pleaded Amy.

"Suppose we take her..." began Meg.

"If she goes *I* won't, and if I don't, *Laurie* won't like it. I would think she'd hate to poke herself in where she isn't wanted," said Jo crossly.

When Laurie called, the two girls hurried down and left their sister crying. As the three set out, Amy called out in a threatening tone, *"You'll be sorry for this, Jo March!"*

Laurie, Jo, and Meg had a charming time, for the play was wonderful. But Jo's pleasure had a drop of bitterness in it. She wondered what her sister would do to make her "sorry."

When they got home, they found Amy reading in the parlor. Jo searched for evidence of Amy's revenge, but everything was in its place. She decided that Amy had forgiven her.

There Jo was mistaken. The next day she made a discovery that produced a storm. Meg, Beth, and Amy were sitting together late in the afternoon when Jo burst into the room. "Has anyone taken my writing book?" she demanded. Meg and Beth said "no" at once, and looked surprised. Amy said nothing. Jo was on her in a minute.

"Amy, you've got it!"

"You'll never see your silly old book again," cried Amy. "I burned it up."

"What! My book I was so fond of, and meant to finish writing before Father got home? Have you really burned it?" said Jo, turning very pale.

"Yes, I did! I told you I'd make you pay yesterday, and I have, so…"

Jo's hot temper took over. She shook Amy till her teeth chattered in her head. "You wicked girl! I never can write it again. I'll never forgive you as long as I live."

When Mrs. March came home she made Amy realize the wrong she had done her sister. Jo's book was the pride of her heart. It was only half a dozen little fairy tales, but Jo had put her whole heart into her work. She had hoped to make something good enough to print. Amy's bonfire had destroyed the loving work of several years.

When the tea bell rang, Jo appeared, looking grim. It took all of Amy's courage to say, "Please forgive me, Jo. I'm very, very sorry."

"I never shall forgive you," was Jo's answer. And from that moment, she ignored Amy entirely.

Next day, Jo still looked like a thunder cloud. "I'll ask Laurie to go skating. He is always kind and jolly," said Jo to herself, and off she went. But Amy heard the clash of skates.

"This is the last ice we shall have," pouted Amy. "But it's no use to ask such a grump to take me."

Meg said, "Go after them. Once Laurie has cheered her up, I'm sure she'll be your friend again."

"I'll try," said Amy.

It was not far to the river. Jo saw Amy coming, and turned her back. Laurie did not see, for he was carefully skating along the shore, testing the ice.

"I'll go on to see if it's all right before we begin to race," Amy heard him say. Jo heard Amy panting after her and so she skated slowly down the river away from Amy.

As Laurie turned the bend, he shouted back, "Keep near the shore. It isn't safe in the middle."

Jo heard, but Amy had not. Jo glanced over her shoulder. "Let her take care of herself," she thought.

Amy skated out toward the smoother ice in the middle of the river. For a minute Jo stood still with a strange feeling in her heart. Then something turned her around—just in time to see Amy go down, with a sudden crash of weak ice and a cry that made Jo's heart freeze.

Jo tried to rush forward, but her feet had no strength. Something rushed swiftly by her, and Laurie's voice cried out, "Bring a rail. Quick!"

Lying flat, Laurie held Amy up by his arm and a hockey stick till Jo dragged a rail from the fence. Together they got the child out, more frightened than hurt. Shivering, dripping, and crying, they got Amy home.

Later, when the house was quiet, Jo went to her mother and said, "If Amy should die, Mother, it would be my fault." She dropped down beside the bed in tears. "It's my dreadful temper! I try to cure it, and then it breaks out worse than ever. Oh, Mother, what shall I do?" cried poor Jo.

"Remember this day, and resolve that you will never know another like it," her mother said. "You think your temper is the worst, but mine used to be just like it."

"Yours, Mother? Why, you are never angry!"

"Your father helped me to control my temper, Jo. He showed me that I must try to practice all the virtues I want my little girls to have."

"Oh, Mother, if I'm ever half as good as you, I'll be satisfied," cried Jo. "I let the sun go down on my anger yesterday. I wouldn't forgive Amy, and today it might have been too late!" She leaned over her sister, softly stroking the wet hair scattered on the pillow.

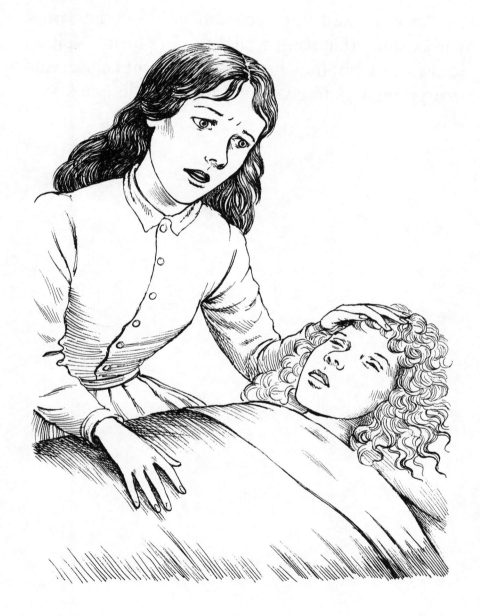

Amy opened her eyes and held out her arms, with a smile that went straight to Jo's heart. Neither said a word, but they hugged one another close. And everything was forgiven and forgotten in one kiss.

CHAPTER NINE

Meg Has a Beauty Lesson

Meg stood packing her trunk one April day. She had been invited to spend two weeks in the country with Annie Moffat and her family. Sallie Gardiner was going as well.

"What did Mother give you out of the treasure box?" asked Amy. The treasure box was a cedar chest in which Mrs. March kept a few old valuables. They were presented as gifts for her girls when the proper time came.

"A pair of silk stockings, that pretty carved fan, and a lovely blue sash. I wanted the violet silk dress, but there isn't time to fix it."

"You've got your white dress for the big party.

You always look like an angel in white," said Amy.

"It will have to do," Meg returned. She looked at her well-worn wardrobe and sighed. "I wonder if I shall *ever* have real lace on my clothes and bows on my caps?"

"You said the other day that you'd be perfectly happy if you could only go to Annie Moffat's," observed Beth in her quiet way.

"So I did! Well, I *am* happy, and I *won't* fret. But it does seem as if the more one gets the more one wants, doesn't it?"

The next day, Meg departed in style for two weeks of pleasure. The Moffats were very fashionable. Simple Meg was rather overwhelmed at first. Everything was so splendid and elegant. But the Moffats were kind people, and soon put their guest at her ease.

Meg certainly liked having nothing to do but enjoy herself. She began to act and talk just like the rich girls around her. The more she saw of Annie's pretty things, the more she sighed to be rich. Home now looked bare and dismal as she thought of it.

It didn't take long for Meg to notice that her own clothing was old and shabby. Annie and her sisters wore only the finest dresses. No one said a word about it, but Meg's heart felt very heavy. She had a gentle heart, but she was also very proud.

Poor Meg did not sleep well after a small party one evening. She got up heavy-eyed and unhappy. That afternoon, Annie's oldest sister, Belle, announced to Meg that she had invited "young Mr. Laurence" to the next big party.

"What shall you wear?" asked Sallie Gardiner.

"My old white dress again," said Meg. She tried to speak quite easily, but felt very uncomfortable.

Belle said kindly, "I've got a sweet blue silk packed away, which I've outgrown. Wear it to please me, won't you?"

"You are very kind. But I don't mind my old dress if you don't," said Meg.

"Now, do let me please myself by dressing you up in style. You'd be a regular little beauty with a touch here and there," said Belle.

Meg agreed. She very much wanted to see if she would be "a little beauty" after some touching up. The excitement caused her to forget all her uncomfortable feelings toward the Moffats.

Belle and her maid turned Meg into a fine lady. They crimped and curled her hair and reddened her lips. They laced her into a sky-blue dress, which was so tight she could hardly breathe. Silver jewelry was added, and a pair of high-heeled silk boots granted the last wish of her heart. A lace handkerchief, a fan, and a bouquet finished her off. Belle proudly looked over her newly dressed doll.

Meg got safely downstairs and into the drawing rooms where the guests had gathered. She very soon discovered that there is a charm about fine clothes. People who had ignored her before were suddenly very polite to her. Young boys asked to meet her.

But soon the tight dress gave her a side-ache. Her skirt kept getting under her feet. And she was afraid she was going to lose or break one of the silver earrings. Then she suddenly saw Laurie. He was staring at her with surprise and disapproval. Something in his honest eyes made her wish she had her old dress on.

Meg crossed the room to shake hands with her friend. "I was afraid you wouldn't come," she said.

"Jo wanted me to come, and tell her how you looked," answered Laurie.

"What shall you tell her?" asked Meg, full of curiosity to know his opinion of her.

"I shall say I didn't know you. For you look so grown-up and unlike yourself, I'm quite afraid of you," he said. "I don't like fuss and feathers."

That was altogether too much from a lad younger than herself. Meg walked away, saying, "You are the rudest boy I ever saw."

She went and stood at a quiet window to cool her cheeks. As she stood there, some of the party guests walked by, but did not see her standing there. Meg heard one of the men say: "They are making such a fool of that March girl. She's made up to look like a doll tonight."

"Oh, dear!" sighed Meg. "I wish I'd been sensible and worn my own things."

Turning, she saw Laurie. He said, "Please forgive my rudeness. Come and dance with me. I don't like your gown, but I do think you are just splendid."

Meg smiled. She whispered, "Take care my skirt doesn't trip you up. I was a goose to wear it."

After the dance, Laurie did not speak to Meg again till suppertime, when he saw her drinking champagne and flirting with Annie's brothers.

"You'll have a splitting headache tomorrow if you drink much of that," he whispered, leaning over her chair.

"I'm not Meg tonight; I'm 'a doll' who does all sorts of crazy things. Tomorrow I shall be good again," she answered.

"Wish tomorrow was here, then," muttered Laurie, unhappy with the change in Meg.

Meg was sick all the next day. On Saturday she went home, feeling that she had "sat in the lap of luxury" long enough. On Sunday evening, she sat with her mother and Jo, saying very little. Then, as the clock struck nine, Meg went to her mother's side, saying bravely, "Marmee, I want to confess."

"I thought so. What is it, dear?"

She told them how the Moffat girls had dressed her up like a doll, and how she had been flattered by the attention. She also confessed to drinking champagne and trying to flirt. Jo saw her mother fold her lips tightly.

Mrs. March said gravely, "I was very unwise to let you go."

"I won't let it hurt me, Mother."

"Learn to know and value the praise which is worth having, Meg."

Meg sighed. "Poor girls don't stand any chance, Belle says."

"Then we'll be old maids," said Jo.

Mrs. March held her daughters' hands. "My dear girls, you do not have to marry rich men merely because they are rich. I'd rather see you poor men's wives, if you were happy, than queens on thrones, without self-respect and peace.

"One thing to remember, my girls: Mother is always ready to be your listening ear, and Father to be your friend. And both of us hope that our daughters will be the pride and comfort of our lives."

"We will, Marmee, we will!" cried both, with all their hearts.

CHAPTER TEN

Spring Ends – And Play Begins

"The first of June! The Kings are off to the seashore tomorrow, and I'm free. Three months' vacation. How I shall enjoy it!" exclaimed Meg.

"Aunt March went today, too!" said Jo. "I was afraid she'd ask me to go with her."

"What shall you do all vacation?" asked Amy.

"I'm going to rest and play to my heart's content," replied Meg.

Jo said, "I'm going to read in the old apple tree."

"Let's not do any lessons for a while, Beth. Let's play all the time and rest," proposed Amy.

"Well, I will, if Mother doesn't mind. I want to learn some new songs," admitted Beth.

"May we, Mother?" asked Meg. Mrs. March sat sewing in the corner.

"You may try your experiment for a week and see how you like it. I think by Saturday night you will find that all play and no work is as bad as all work and no play."

They began by lounging for the rest of the day. Next morning, Meg did not appear till ten o'clock. The room seemed lonely and untidy. Jo had not filled the vases, Beth had not dusted, and Amy's books lay scattered about. Nothing was neat and pleasant but Marmee's corner.

Jo spent the morning on the river with Laurie and the afternoon reading up in the apple tree. Beth went to her music. Amy sat down to draw under the honeysuckle. She got caught in a rain shower and came home dripping. Meg went shopping in the afternoon.

At tea time they met to discuss their day. Meg had discovered her new dress would shrink in the wash. Jo had sunburned her nose and had a raging headache. Beth was weary from learning three or four songs at once. Amy deeply regretted the rain damage done to her dress.

But these were small troubles. They assured

their mother that the experiment was working fine. She smiled and said nothing. With Hannah's help she did their neglected work.

It was amazing how uncomfortable things became. The days got longer and longer. Everyone felt uneasy. Meg spoiled her clothes in her attempts to fancy them up. Jo got so fidgety that even Laurie quarreled with her. Beth got on pretty well, for she was constantly forgetting that it was to be *all play and no work*. Amy fared worst of all. She didn't like dolls, fairy tales were childish, and one couldn't draw *all* the time.

By Friday night each was glad the week was nearly done. Hoping to help them learn their lesson more deeply, Mrs. March gave Hannah a vacation. She wanted the girls to enjoy the full effect of the experiment. When they got up Saturday morning, there was no fire in the kitchen, and no breakfast in the dining room. Their mother was nowhere to be seen.

"Mercy on us! What *has* happened?" cried Jo.

"Mother says she is going to stay quietly in her room all day," said Meg, coming downstairs. "She says it has been a hard week for her. We must take care of ourselves."

It was an immense relief to have a little work. There was plenty of food in the pantry. While Beth and Amy set the table, Meg made breakfast.

Jo took a tray up to their mother. The boiled tea was very bitter, the omelet scorched, and the biscuits tough. But Mrs. March received them with thanks. She laughed heartily after Jo was gone.

Many were the complaints below about the awful breakfast. "Never mind, I'll get the lunch," said Jo, who knew less than Meg about cooking. With perfect faith in her own powers as a chef, she immediately invited Laurie to lunch.

Jo walked to the market. She was sure she made very good bargains. She bought a very young lobster, some very old asparagus, and two boxes of unripe strawberries.

Mrs. March went out, after peeping here and there to see how matters went. A strange sense of helplessness fell upon the girls as the gray bonnet vanished round the corner.

Words cannot describe Jo's attempts at cooking. She boiled the asparagus until the tops fell apart. The bread burned black. She hammered and poked the little lobster and hid the small bits of meat in lettuce leaves. The potatoes were not done.

"It's terrible to spend your whole morning for nothing," thought Jo. She rang the bell half an hour later than usual.

One thing after another was tasted and left on the plates. Amy giggled and Meg looked distressed. Laurie talked and laughed to give a cheerful tone to the scene.

Jo's one strong point was the fruit. She knew she had sugared it well, and had a pitcher of rich cream to eat with it. She glanced at Laurie. There was a slight pucker around his mouth. Amy took a heaping spoonful, choked, hid her face in her napkin, and left the table quickly.

"Oh, what is it?" exclaimed Jo.

"Salt instead of sugar, and the cream is sour," replied Meg.

Jo uttered a groan and fell back in her chair. She was on the verge of crying when she met Laurie's eyes, which looked merry. The comical side of the affair suddenly struck her, and she laughed till tears ran down her cheeks. The unfortunate lunch ended happily, with bread and butter, olives and fun.

As twilight fell, the girls gathered on the porch where the June roses were budding beautifully. Each groaned or sighed as she sat down, as if tired or troubled.

"Are you pleased with your experiment, girls?" Marmee asked, as Beth nestled up to her. They each turned toward Mother with brightening faces, as flowers turn toward the sun.

"Not me!" cried Jo decidedly.

"Nor I," echoed the others.

"You think that it is better to have a few duties and live a little for others, do you?"

"Lounging doesn't pay," observed Jo. "I'm tired of it."

"Work is wholesome," Marmee said. "It keeps us from mischief, is good for health and spirits, and gives us a sense of independence."

"We'll work like busy bees, see if we don't," said Jo. "I'll learn cooking, and my next dinner party will be a success."

"I'll make a set of shirts for Father. That will be better than fussing over my own things," said Meg.

"I'll do my lessons every day, and not spend so much time with my music," said Beth.

Amy followed their example by declaring, "I shall learn to make buttonholes, and attend to my grammar lessons."

"Very good! Then I am quite satisfied with the experiment. Remember to have regular hours for work and play, and make each day both useful and pleasant."

"We'll remember, Mother!"

And they did.

CHAPTER ELEVEN

A *Summer Picnic*

Laurie invited the March girls to join him on a picnic. Some friends of his from England were visiting, and he hoped to show them a grand time.

Jo flew in to tell the news. "Of course we can go—Mother? Laurie's tutor, Mr. Brooke, is going as the chaperone. Ned Moffat and Sallie Gardiner are coming, too. I can row, and Meg can see to lunch."

"Do you know anything about the English family, Jo?" asked Meg.

"Only that there are four of them. Kate is older than you. Fred and Frank—twins—are about my age. And there is a little girl, Grace, who is nine or ten. Laurie knew them in Europe."

Jo turned to her sister. "You'll come, Bethy?"

"If you won't let any boys talk to me. I like to please Laurie, and I'm not afraid of Mr. Brooke, he is so kind. But I don't want to play, or sing, or say anything."

"That's my good girl. You do try to fight off your shyness, and I love you for it. Fighting faults isn't easy, as I know. Now let's do double duty today, so that we can play tomorrow with free minds," said Jo, picking up a broom.

The sun peeped into the girls' room early next morning, and soon a lively bustle began in both houses. Beth kept looking out the window and reporting what went on next door.

"There goes the man with the tent! Now Mr. Laurence is looking up at the sky. I wish he would go, too. There's Laurie, looking like a sailor! Oh, here's a carriage full of people—a tall lady, a little girl, and two dreadful boys. One is lame. Poor thing, he's got a crutch. Be quick, girls! It's getting late."

Jo marched straight away and the rest followed. They were a bright little band of sisters, all looking their best in summer suits, with happy faces under their bouncy hat brims.

Laurie ran to meet the girls and present them to his friends. Meg was grateful to see that Miss Kate was dressed simply. Jo thought Kate had a stand-off-don't-touch-me air. Beth decided that the lame boy, Frank, was not "dreadful," but gentle, and she would be kind to him. Amy found Grace a well-mannered, merry little person. After staring at one another for a few minutes, they suddenly became very good friends.

The group set off in two rowboats, and Fred manned a wherry boat. It was not far to the picnic field. The tent was pitched and the croquet wickets were down by the time they arrived.

"Welcome to Camp Laurence!" said the young host as they landed with exclamations of delight. "Let's have a game before it gets hot, and then we'll see about dinner."

Frank, Beth, Amy, and Grace sat down to watch the game played by the other eight. Mr. Brooke chose Meg, Kate, and Fred. Laurie took Sallie, Jo, and Ned. The English played well, but the Americans played better.

Fred cheated a bit, and Jo got angry, but managed to keep her temper. Both Meg and Laurie praised her for it.

Mr. Brooke, who was Laurie's tutor, had come along to watch over the young crowd. Meg had noticed that he was an intelligent, warm man with handsome brown eyes.

Mr. Brooke looked at his watch and announced, "Time for lunch."

A very merry lunch it was, for everything seemed fresh and funny.

"What shall we do when we can't eat any more?" asked Laurie.

"Have games till it's cooler," returned Jo. "I dare say Miss Kate knows something new and nice. Go and ask her. She's company, and you ought to stay with her more."

"Aren't you company, too? I thought Kate would suit Brooke, but he keeps talking to Meg."

Miss Kate *did* know several new games. They first tried something called Rig-marole. One person began a story, and told it as long as they pleased. Then, just at some exciting point, the next person took over the story. The happy group told a most outrageous and interesting story. Afterward, the elders—Meg, Kate, and Mr. Brooke—sat together on the grass. Miss Kate took out her sketch book.

"I wish I could draw," said Meg.

"Why don't you learn?" returned Miss Kate.

"I haven't time."

"I took a few lessons privately. Can't you do the same with your governess?"

"I have none. I am a governess myself."

"Oh, indeed!" said Miss Kate. But she might as well have said, "Dear me, how dreadful!"

Mr. Brooke looked up and said quickly, "Young ladies in America are admired and respected for supporting themselves."

"Oh, yes, of course it's very nice and proper in America for them to do so," said Miss Kate in a rather rude voice.

Mr. Brooke had recently translated a German song for Meg, and he asked her if she had found his work useful. The two of them studied a little book of German poetry together. Miss Kate watched them closely. Then she shut her sketchbook, saying, "I must look after Grace." She strolled away, adding to herself, "What odd people these Yankees are. I'm afraid Laurie will be quite spoiled among them."

"I forgot that English people turn up their noses at governesses," said Meg to Mr. Brooke when Kate had left.

"There's no place like America for us workers, Miss Margaret," said Mr. Brooke, looking quite cheerful.

"I'm glad I live in it then. I only wish I liked teaching as you do."

"I think you would if you had Laurie for a student. I shall be very sorry to lose him next year," said Mr. Brooke.

"Going to college, I suppose?" Meg's lips asked that question, but her eyes added, "And what becomes of you?"

"Yes, it's high time he went. As soon as he is off, I shall become a soldier."

"I am glad of that!" exclaimed Meg. "I should think every young man would want to go help in the war. Though it is hard for the mothers and sisters who stay at home," she added sorrowfully.

"I have no mother or sisters," said Mr. Brooke in a quiet voice.

"Laurie and his grandfather would care a great deal if you went. And we would all be very sorry to have any harm happen to you," said Meg, looking into those handsome brown eyes.

"Thank you," returned Mr. Brooke, looking into Meg's eyes, and becoming cheerful again.

Another game of croquet finished the afternoon. At sunset the tent was taken down, baskets packed, wickets pulled up, and boats loaded. The whole party floated down the river, singing at the tops of their voices.

On the lawn where it had gathered, the little party separated. As the four sisters went home through the garden, Miss Kate looked after them. She said quite smugly, "In spite of their strange manners, American girls are very nice when one knows them."

"I quite agree with you," said Mr. Brooke.

CHAPTER TWELVE

Castles in the Air

Laurie was swinging in his hammock one warm September afternoon when he saw the Marches going out on some journey.

"Well, that's cool," said Laurie to himself. "To have a picnic and never ask me! I'll see what's going on."

He topped the hill the girls had climbed and peeped through the bushes. "Here's a scene!" he said to himself.

It *was* a pretty picture. The sisters sat together in a shady nook, with sun and shadow flickering over them. The wind lifted their hair and cooled their hot cheeks. Meg sat sewing daintily and looking as fresh

and sweet as a rose. Beth was sorting pinecones, for she made pretty things with them. Amy was sketching a group of ferns. Jo was knitting as she read aloud.

"May I come in, please? Or shall I be a bother?" Laurie asked, advancing slowly.

Meg lifted her eyebrows, but Jo scowled at her. She said at once, "Of course you may. We should have asked you before, only we thought you wouldn't care for such a girl's game."

"I always like your games. But if Meg doesn't want me, I'll go away."

"I don't mind, if you do something. It's against the rules to be lazy here. If you want to join the 'Busy Bee Society,' you must be useful," said Meg.

"Mother likes to have us out-of-doors as much as possible. We bring our work here and have nice times," said Jo. "From this hill we can see far away to the place where we hope to live sometime."

Jo pointed, and Laurie sat up to examine. Through an opening in the wood one could look across the wide, blue river, far over the outskirts of the great city, to the green hills that rose to meet the sky. The sun was low, and the heavens glowed with the beauty of an autumn sunset.

"How beautiful that is!" said Laurie softly.

"Wouldn't it be fun if all our dreams and castles in the air could come true, and we could live in them?" said Jo.

"I'd be a famous musician," said Laurie. "And I'd never be bothered about money or business. I'd just enjoy myself and live for what I like. That's my favorite castle. What's yours, Meg?"

Meg found it hard to tell hers. She said slowly, "I would like a lovely house, full of beautiful things. Nice food, pretty clothes, handsome furniture, and heaps of money. How I should enjoy it!"

Jo said, "I want to do something heroic or wonderful that won't be forgotten after I'm dead. I think I shall write books, and get rich and famous. That would suit me, so that is *my* favorite dream."

"Mine is to stay at home safe, and help take care of the family," said Beth with a content smile. "Since I have my little piano, I am perfectly satisfied. I only wish we may all keep well and be together. Nothing else."

"I have ever so many wishes. But my favorite is to be an artist, and go to Rome. I'll do fine pictures, and be the best artist in the whole world," was Amy's modest desire.

"In ten years let's meet, and see how many of us have got our wishes. Or how much nearer we are then than now," said Jo.

"I hope I shall have done something to be proud of by that time. But I'm such a lazy dog," Laurie admitted. "Grandfather wants me to be a businessman, and I'd rather be shot."

Meg said in her most motherly tone, "Do your best at college, Laurie. Then your grandfather won't be unfair to you. Do your duty and you'll get your reward by being respected and loved. Good Mr. Brooke has done his duty, and he will be rewarded in some way, I'm sure."

"What do *you* know about Mr. Brooke?" asked Laurie. His black eyes twinkled slyly.

Meg blushed. "Only what your grandpa told us about him. He took care of his own mother till she died. Now he helps to support the old woman who nursed his mother. He is just as generous and patient and good as he can be."

"So he is, dear fellow!" said Laurie heartily. "It's like Grandpa to find out all about him, and to tell his goodness to others. If ever I do get my wish, you'll see what I do for Brooke."

Laurie squeezed Meg's kind little hand. To show he was not offended by her lecture, he wound yarn for her. Then he recited poetry to please Jo, shook down cones for Beth, and helped Amy with her ferns. In all, he proved himself well fit for the "Busy Bee Society."

That night, when Beth played the piano for Mr. Laurence, Laurie watched the old man, who sat with his gray head on his hand.

The boy said to himself, "I'll let my castle go, and stay with the dear old gentleman while he needs me. I am all he has."

CHAPTER THIRTEEN

Autumn Secrets

The autumn sun lay warmly in the high window. Jo was seated on the old sofa in the attic, writing busily, her papers spread out before her.

She scribbled away till the last page was filled, then signed her name with a fancy flair. She threw down her pen, and exclaimed, "There, I've done my best!"

Jo tied the papers up with a red ribbon. She took another set of papers from the cupboard, and put both in her pocket. Then she crept downstairs.

Very quietly, Jo put on her hat and jacket. Going to the back window, she got out on the roof of a low porch. She swung herself down and took a roundabout way to the road. Once there, she hailed a passing carriage-bus. She looked very merry and mysterious as it rolled away.

The bus let her off in town, and after a few wrong turns, she found the place she was looking for. She went into the doorway and looked up the dirty stairs. After standing still a minute, she suddenly walked away. She went back, stood, and walked away again several times. This greatly amused a black-eyed young gentleman who was watching her from the window of a building across the street. Finally Jo gave herself a shake, pulled her hat over her eyes, and walked up the stairs. She looked scared and nervous, as if she were going to have all her teeth out.

There was a dentist's sign, among others, at the entrance to the building. The young gentleman stared at the sign for a moment. Then he put on his coat and went down to wait in the doorway.

In ten minutes Jo came running downstairs with a very red face. When she saw the young gentleman she looked anything but pleased. He asked, "Did you have a bad time?"

"Not very."

"How many did you have out?"

Jo looked at her friend as if she did not understand him, then began to laugh. He thought she had been to the dentist!

"What are you laughing at?" said Laurie.

They walked in silence a few minutes. Then Laurie said, "I'd like to tell you something very interesting. It's a secret. If I tell you, you must tell me *your* secret."

Jo thought about this for a moment. Then she whispered, "Well, I've left two stories with a newspaper man to see if he'll print them. He will give me his answer next week."

"Hooray for Miss March, the famous American author!" cried Laurie. "Your stories are works of Shakespeare compared to half the rubbish that is published every day."

Jo's eyes sparkled. "And what's *your* secret?"

"I know where Meg's other glove is."

"Is that all?" said Jo, looking disappointed. Meg had left a pair of gloves at the Laurences' house weeks ago. Only one had ever been found. Laurie nodded with a face full of mystery. "All right, Laurie, tell then. Where's the glove?"

Laurie bent, and whispered three words in Jo's ear. She looked shocked and quite displeased.

"How do you know?" Jo said sharply.

"Saw it in his pocket. Isn't it romantic?"

"No! It's horrid!"

"Don't you like the secret?"

"Of course I don't. The idea of anybody coming to take Meg away! No, thank you," said Jo rather ungratefully. She tried to hide the trembling of her lips. Lately she had felt that Meg was getting to be a woman, and Laurie's secret made her dread the separation which now seemed very near.

For a week or two, Jo behaved so strangely that her sisters were quite bewildered. She rushed to the door when the postman rang. She was rude to Mr. Brooke whenever they met. And she sat looking at Meg with a sad face.

Two weeks after Jo's secret trip to town, Meg saw Laurie chasing Jo all over the garden. Shrieks of laughter were heard.

In a few minutes Jo bounced into the parlor. She laid herself on the sofa and pretended to read the newspaper.

"Anything interesting?" asked Meg.

"Nothing but a story," returned Jo.

"Read it aloud. That will keep you out of mischief," said Amy in her most grown-up tone.

"What's the name of the story?" asked Beth, wondering why Jo kept her face behind the paper.

"*The Rival Painters.*"

"That sounds well. Read it," said Meg.

Jo began to read very fast. The girls listened with interest, for the tale was romantic and somewhat sad. Most of the characters died.

"Who wrote it?" asked Beth, who had caught a glimpse of Jo's face.

The reader suddenly sat up, cast away the paper, and replied in a loud voice, "Your sister!"

"You?" cried Meg, dropping her work.

"It's very good," said Amy critically.

"I knew it! Oh, my Jo, I *am* so proud!" Beth ran to hug her sister.

How delighted they all were, to be sure! How Meg wouldn't believe it till she saw the words "Miss Josephine March" actually printed in the paper. How kindly Amy remarked on the artistic parts of the story. How Beth skipped and sang with joy. How proud Mrs. March was when she knew it. How Jo laughed, with tears in her eyes.

Jo told of her adventure to see the newspaper man. She explained how she had been waiting all this time to see if one of her stories would be printed. She added, "And when I went to get my answer, he said he liked them both. He doesn't pay beginners, only lets them print in his paper. So I let him have the two stories. I shall write more, and he's going to pay me for the next one. I *am* so happy, for I may be able to support myself and help the girls."

Jo's breath gave out. Wrapping her head in the paper, she shed a few tears. To earn her own money and earn the praise of those she loved were the dearest wishes of her heart. This seemed to be the first step toward that happy end.

CHAPTER FOURTEEN

The Telegram

"November is so dreary," grumbled Meg as she stood at the window one dull afternoon, looking out at the frostbitten garden. "And nothing pleasant *ever* happens here."

Beth sat at the other window. She said, "Two pleasant things are going to happen right away. Marmee is coming down the street. And Laurie is coming through the garden as if he had something nice to tell."

In they both came. Mrs. March asked her usual question, "Any letter from Father, girls?" And Laurie asked, "Won't some of you come for a drive?"

"Laurie, will you call at the post office?" asked Mrs. March as the girls went off for their coats. "It's our day for a letter."

A sharp ring of the door bell interrupted her. A minute later Hannah came in with a telegram.

Mrs. March read the two lines it contained and dropped back into her chair. It was as if the little paper had sent a bullet to her heart. Jo read aloud in a frightened voice:

Mrs. March:
Your husband is very ill. Come at once.
                    S. Hale
Blank Hospital, Washington

How still the room was as they listened. How strangely the day darkened. How suddenly the whole world seemed to change, as the girls gathered about their mother. They felt as if all the happiness and support of their lives was about to be taken from them.

Mrs. March stretched out her arms to her daughters. "I shall go at once," she said. "But it may be too late. Oh, children, help me to bear it!"

For several minutes there was nothing but the sound of sobbing in the room. They tried to be calm as their mother sat up. Looking pale but steady, she put away her grief to think and plan.

"Laurie, send a telegram saying I will come at once. The next train goes early in the morning. I'll take that. And please leave a note at Aunt March's. Jo, give me that pen and paper."

Jo knew what her mother was about to do. She would need money for the journey, and she must ask to borrow it from Aunt March. Her mother quickly made a list of errands, and Jo scurried out of the house.

Mr. Laurence hurried over to say how sad he was at the news. He offered to escort Mrs. March to Washington. Mrs. March thanked him kindly, but would not hear of that. Mr. Laurence marched off, saying he'd be back soon. No one thought of him again until Meg suddenly came upon Mr. Brooke in the door entry.

"I came to offer myself as escort to your mother," he said in a warm, quiet voice.

Meg put out her hand. "How kind you are! It will be such a relief to know she has someone to take care of her. Thank you very, very much!"

The short afternoon wore away. Jo had not been seen for hours, when at last she came walking in with a very odd expression. She handed a roll of money to her mother. "That's my part toward making Father comfortable and bringing him home!"

"Twenty-five dollars! Jo, I hope you haven't done anything rash."

"No, I only sold something that was my own."

As she spoke, Jo took off her bonnet. Everyone gasped, for her flowing hair was cut short.

"Your hair! Your beautiful hair!"

"Oh, Jo, how could you?"

"My dear girl, there was no need of this."

Jo rumpled her hair, trying to look as if she liked it. "It will do my brains good to have that mop taken off. My head feels so light and cool."

"What made you do it?" asked Amy, who would have cut off her head before cutting her pretty hair.

"Well, I was wild to do something for Father," replied Jo, as they gathered about the table. "I saw the barber shop and knew what I had to do. The woman there picked out a long lock for me to keep. I'll give it to you, Marmee."

Mrs. March put the wavy chestnut lock away with a short gray one in her desk. She only said, "Thank you, deary," but something in her face made the girls change the subject. They talked as cheerfully as they could about the happy times they would have when Father came home.

No one wanted to go to bed that evening. Finally Mrs. March put away her sewing and said, "Come girls." Beth went to the piano and played their father's favorite hymn. All began bravely, but broke down one by one till Beth was left alone, singing with all her heart.

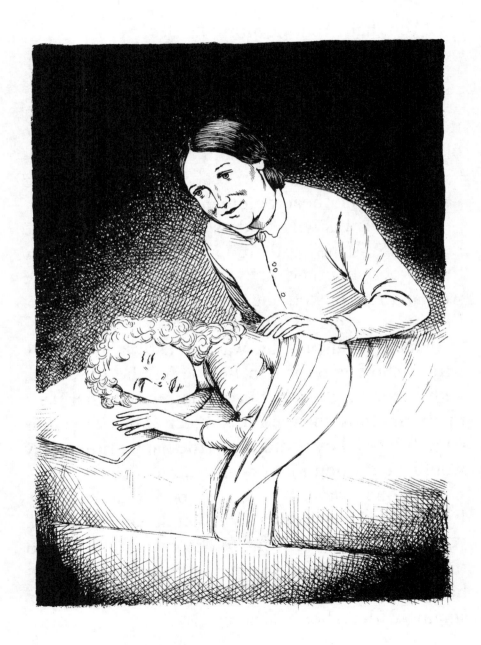

The clocks were striking midnight and the rooms were very still as a figure glided quietly from bed to bed. It smoothed a cover here and settled a pillow there, looking tenderly at each sleeping face. It kissed each, and prayed as only a mother can.

Mrs. March lifted the curtain. The moon came from behind the clouds and shone upon her like a kind face that seemed to whisper, "Be comforted, dear soul! There is always light behind the clouds."

As they dressed in the cold, gray dawn, the sisters agreed to say good-bye cheerfully and send their mother on her journey without tears.

The big trunk stood ready in the hall. Mother's cloak and bonnet lay on the sofa. Mother sat trying to eat, but looking pale and worn. Meg's eyes kept filling with tears. Jo hid her face more than once. The little girls wore troubled expressions.

As they waited for the carriage Mrs. March said to the girls, "Hope and keep busy. Visit the poor Hummels. Meg, watch over your sisters, and in any trouble go to Mr. Laurence. Be patient, Jo, and be my brave girl. Beth, comfort yourself with your music and help around the house. And you, Amy, help all you can, and keep happy, safe at home."

"We will, Mother! We will!"

The carriage approached with a rattle. That was the hardest minute. No one cried, though their hearts were very heavy. They kissed their mother quietly and clung about her tenderly.

Laurie and his grandfather came over to see her off. Mr. Brooke looked so strong and kind that the girls named him "Mr. Greatheart" on the spot.

"Good-bye, my darlings! God bless and keep us all!" whispered Mrs. March. She kissed one dear little face after the other, and hurried into the carriage. The girls tried to wave their hands cheerfully. As she rolled away, the sun came out. Looking back, she saw it shining on the group at the gate like a good sign.

CHAPTER FIFTEEN

A Bitter Winter Wind

For a week, everyone seemed in a heavenly frame of mind. Good news about their father comforted the girls very much. Mr. Brooke sent a letter every day, which grew more cheerful as the week passed. At first the girls were very well-behaved and serious. But as the news kept getting better, they began to fall back into their old ways.

Jo caught a bad cold and was ordered to stay at home till she was better. Amy grew bored with housework and returned to her art. Meg wrote long letters to her mother. Beth visited the Hummels and performed her little duties faithfully each day—and even some of her sisters'.

They all felt that they had done well and deserved praise. And so they did, but then they stopped doing well—and learned a hard lesson.

"Meg, I wish you'd go and see the Hummels. You know Mother told us not to forget them," said Beth. It had been ten days since Mrs. March had left.

"I'm too tired to go this afternoon," replied Meg, rocking comfortably.

"Can't you, Jo?' asked Beth.

"Too stormy for me with my cold," said Jo.

"Why don't you go yourself?" asked Meg.

"I have been every day. But the baby is sick, and I don't know what to do for it. It gets sicker and sicker. I think you or Hannah ought to go."

Meg promised she would go tomorrow.

So Beth quietly put on her hood, filled her basket with treats for the poor children, and went out into the chilly air. It was late when she came back. No one saw her creep upstairs and shut herself into her mother's room. Half an hour after, Jo found little Beth, looking very ill, her eyes red.

"What's the matter?" cried Jo.

Beth put out her hand as if to warn her off. She whispered quickly, "You've had the scarlet fever, haven't you, Jo?"

"Years ago, when Meg did. Why?"

"Oh, Jo, Mrs. Hummel's baby is dead! It died in my lap before she got home," cried Beth with a sob.

"My poor dear, how dreadful for you!" said Jo. She took her sister in her arms as she sat down.

"When I got there Mrs. Hummel had gone for a doctor. The baby seemed asleep, but all of a sudden if gave a little cry and trembled, and then lay very still. I knew it was dead."

"Don't cry, dear! What did you do?"

"I just sat and held it softly till Mrs. Hummel came with the doctor. He said it was dead, and that it was scarlet fever. He told me to go home and take medicine right away, or I'd have it."

"Oh, Beth, if you should be sick I never could forgive myself! What shall we do?" cried Jo with a frightened look. She hugged her close. "If Mother was only at home!" she said. "You've been with the baby every day for more than a week, so I'm afraid you are going to have it, Beth. I'll call Hannah. She knows all about sickness."

Hannah assured them that there was no need to worry. Everyone got scarlet fever, and if rightly treated, nobody died.

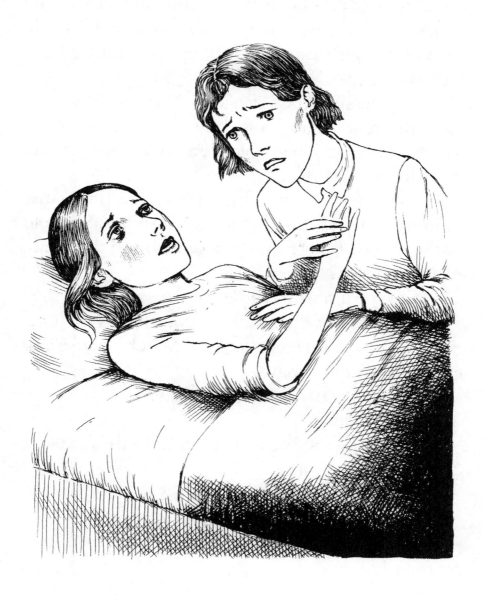

"We will have Dr. Bangs just take a look at you, dear," she said. "Then we'll send Amy off so she won't catch the fever. She can stay with Aunt March. One of you girls can stay at home and amuse Beth for a day or two."

Amy passionately declared that she'd rather have the fever than go to stay with grumpy Aunt March. Meg reasoned, pleaded, and commanded, but still Amy refused.

Laurie walked into the parlor to find Amy sobbing with her head in the sofa cushions. She told her story, but Laurie only walked around the room, whistling softly.

"Now be a sensible little woman, and do as they say," he urged her gently. "Scarlet fever is no joke, miss. I promise I'll come to Aunt March's house and take you out every day."

"Will you come every single day?"

"See if I don't."

"And bring me back the minute Beth is well?"

"The very minute."

"Well—I guess I will go," said Amy slowly.

"Good girl! Call Meg, and tell her you'll give in."

Meg and Jo came running down, and Amy promised to go.

"What a difficult world it is!" said Jo. "No sooner do we get out of one trouble than down comes another. I'm lost with Mother gone."

"I think we ought to tell her if Beth is really ill. But Hannah says Mother can't leave Father, and it will only make them anxious," worried Meg. "Jo, go and get Dr. Bangs at once. We can't decide anything till he has been."

Dr. Bangs came and said Beth had symptoms of the fever, but he thought she would have it lightly. Amy was ordered off to Aunt March's house.

CHAPTER SIXTEEN

Dark Days

Beth was much sicker than anyone imagined. Meg stayed at home so she would not infect the King children. She felt guilty when she wrote letters to Washington and did not tell anything about Beth's illness.

Jo devoted herself to Beth day and night. It was not a hard task, for Beth was a sweet and tender patient. But there came a time during the fever when she began to talk in a hoarse, broken voice. She played on the bed cover as if on her beloved little piano. She did not know the familiar faces around her, but called them by wrong names. She also called for her mother.

Jo grew frightened. Meg begged to write the truth. A letter from Washington added to their trouble. Mr. March had grown sicker and could not come home for a long while.

The days seemed dark now. The sisters were sad and lonely as they worked and waited, while the shadow of death hovered. Meg often sat alone with tears dropping on her work. She thought about how rich she had been in things more precious than anything money could buy—love, peace, and health. These were the real blessings of life.

Living in the darkened sick room, Jo learned to see the beauty and sweetness of Beth's nature. She felt how deep and tender a place she filled in all hearts. She realized the worth of Beth's goal to live for others and make home happy.

And Amy longed to be at home. She felt that no work would be troublesome. She grew sad as she remembered how many tasks Beth's willing hands had done for her.

Laurie haunted the house like a restless ghost. Mr. Laurence sadly locked the grand piano.

Everyone missed Beth. The milkman, baker, grocer, and butcher asked how she did. Neighbors sent all sorts of comforts and good wishes. Even the

sisters were surprised to find how many friends Beth had made.

Dr. Bangs came twice a day. Hannah sat up at night. Meg kept a telegram in her desk ready to send off at any minute, and Jo never stirred from Beth's side.

The first of December, a bitter wind blew, snow fell fast, and the year seemed getting ready for its death. When Dr. Bangs came that morning, he looked long at Beth. He held her hot hand in his own, then laid it gently down.

"If Mrs. March can leave her husband she'd better be sent for," he said in a low voice.

Meg dropped down into a chair. Jo ran to the parlor, snatched up the telegram, and rushed out into the storm.

After Jo returned, Laurie came in with a letter from the post office saying that Mr. March was mending again. Jo's face was so full of misery that Laurie asked quickly, "Is Beth worse?"

"I've sent for Mother," said Jo.

"Oh, Jo, it's not so bad as that?" cried Laurie.

"Yes, it is. She doesn't know who we are. She doesn't look like my Beth, and there's nobody to help us bear it!"

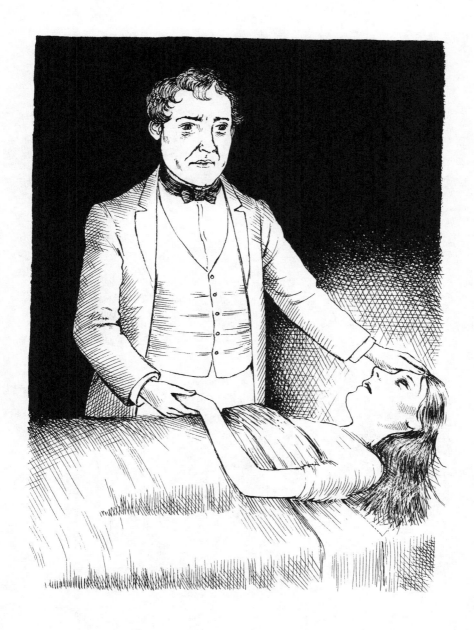

As the tears streamed down poor Jo's cheeks, she stretched out her hand. Laurie took it in his, whispering as well as he could with a lump in his throat, "I'm here. Hold on to me, Jo, dear!"

The warm grasp of his hand comforted Jo's sore heart. She cried miserably, and Laurie drew his hand across his eyes. As Jo's sobs quieted, he said hopefully, "I don't think she will die. She's so good, and we all love her so much. I don't believe God will take her away yet."

"The good and dear people always do die," groaned Jo. But she stopped crying, for her friend's words cheered her up in spite of her own doubts and fears.

"Poor girl, you're worn out. I'll hearten you up in a jiffy. Tonight I'll give you something that will warm your heart," said Laurie, beaming at her.

"What is it?" cried Jo.

"I secretly telegraphed your mother yesterday, and Brooke answered she'd come at once. She'll be here tonight, and everything will be all right. The late train is in at two in the morning."

Laurie spoke very fast and turned red and excited. Jo grew quite white and threw her arms round his neck, crying, "Oh, Laurie! I am so glad!"

Everyone rejoiced but Beth. She lay in a deep sleep. She woke only now and then to mutter, "Water!" All day Jo and Meg hovered over her, and all day the snow fell, the bitter wind raged, and the hours dragged slowly by.

Night came at last. The doctor had said that some change, for better or worse, would probably take place about midnight. Hannah lay down on the sofa. Mr. Laurence paced in the parlor. Laurie lay on the rug, staring into the fire.

The clock struck twelve, and Meg and Jo thought a change passed over Beth's face. An hour went by, and nothing happened except Laurie's quiet departure for the station. Another hour, still no one came. Fears of delay in the storm, or accidents—or, worst of all, a great grief in Washington—haunted the girls.

It was past two when Jo heard a movement by the bed. Turning quickly, she saw Meg kneeling before their mother's chair with her face hidden. A dreadful fear passed coldly over Jo as she thought, "Beth is dead, and Meg is afraid to tell me." A great change seemed to have taken place. The fever flush and the look of pain were gone, and the beloved little face looked peaceful.

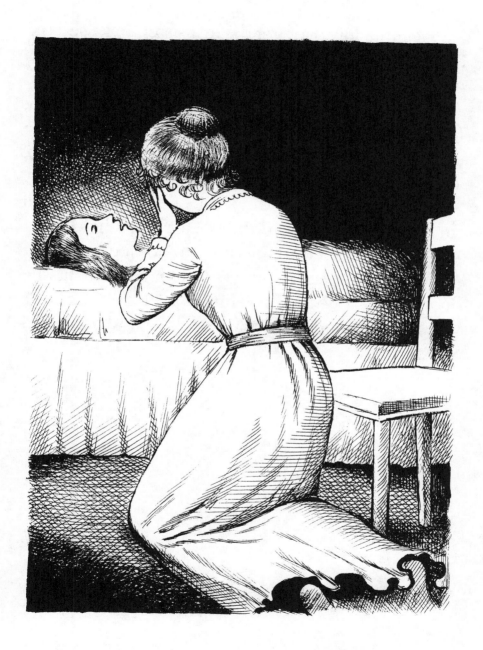

Leaning low over her dearest sister, Jo kissed the damp forehead. She whispered softly, "Good-bye, my Beth. Good-bye!"

Hannah hurried to the bed. She looked at Beth, felt her hands, and listened at her lips. Then she exclaimed, "The fever's turned. Her skin's damp, and she breathes easy. Praise be given!"

"Yes, my dears, I think the little girl will pull through this time," said the doctor when he came.

"Listen!" cried Jo, jumping to her feet.

Yes, there was a sound of carriage bells at the door below, a cry from Hannah, and then Laurie's voice saying in a joyful whisper, "Girls, she's come! She's come!"

There was color and life in the boy's face now.
The girl was better than a doctor.

Belle proudly looked over her newly dressed doll.

Amy sat down to draw under the honeysuckle.

"Everyone looks so happy now. I don't believe they could be much improved."

CHAPTER SEVENTEEN

A *Mother's Touch*

Words cannot describe the meeting of mother and daughters. The house filled with happiness. When Beth woke, the first thing she saw was her mother's face. She smiled and nestled close in the loving arms about her. Then she slept again. The girls waited upon their mother, for she would not unclasp the thin hand that clung to hers even in sleep.

Hannah served an astonishing breakfast, and Meg and Jo fed their mother like young storks. They listened to her whispered account of Father's health and Mr. Brooke's promise to stay with him. She told of the delays caused by the storm on the

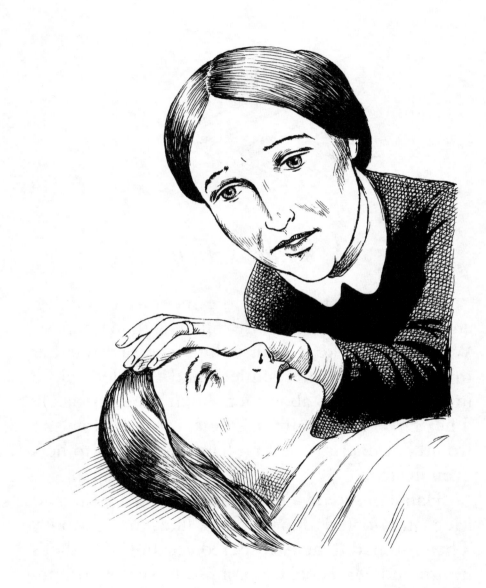

journey home, and the comfort Laurie's face had given her when she arrived at the station.

What a strange yet pleasant day that was. So brilliant and happy outside, for everyone seemed to be out welcoming the first snow. So quiet and restful inside, for everyone slept, and there was a stillness throughout the house. Mrs. March would not leave Beth's side. She rested in the big chair, waking often to look at and touch her child.

Laurie meanwhile set off for Aunt March's house to comfort Amy. Aunt March and Amy both had tears in their eyes when they heard the good news. By then, Laurie was tired from his long night, so Amy persuaded him to rest on the sofa.

Laurie was wakened later by Amy's cry of joy at the sight of her mother. There probably were a good many happy little girls in the city that day, but Amy was the happiest of all. She sat in her mother's lap and told her of her adventures with Aunt March and her pet parrot. Marmee saw something on Amy's hand that made her smile.

Amy said gravely, "Aunt gave me this turquoise ring today. She called me to her and kissed me, and put it on my finger, and said I was a credit to her. I'd like to wear it, Mother. Can I?"

"It's very pretty. But I think you're a little too young for such decorations, Amy," said Mrs. March. She looked down at the plump little hand with the band of sky-blue stones on the finger.

"I don't like it only because it's so pretty," said Amy. "I want to wear it to remind me of something. Beth isn't selfish, and that's the reason everyone loves her. I'm going to try and be like Beth all I can. If I had something always around me to remind me, I would do better. May we try this way?"

"Wear your ring, dear, and do your best. I think you will succeed, for the sincere wish to be good is half the battle. Now I must go back to Beth. Keep up your heart, little daughter, and we will soon have you home again."

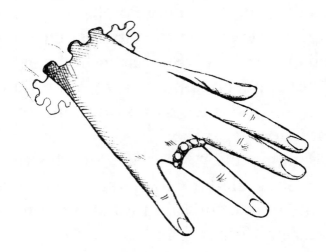

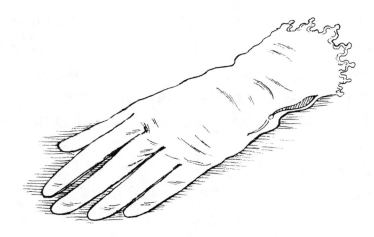

That evening Jo slipped upstairs into Beth's room. Marmee was in her usual place by the bed. Jo stood a minute, twisting her fingers in her hair with a worried look.

"What is it, deary?" asked Mrs. March, holding out her hand.

"I want to tell you something, Mother. Last summer Meg left a pair of gloves at the Laurences' and only one was returned. Now Laurie has told me that Mr. Brooke keeps it as a reminder of Meg. He said Mr. Brooke liked Meg but didn't dare say so, since she was so young and he so poor. Now, isn't it a dreadful state of things?"

"Do you think Meg cares for him?" asked Mrs. March.

"Mercy me! I don't know anything about love and such nonsense!" cried Jo. "In novels, girls blush, faint away, grow thin, and act like fools. But Meg looks so calm when I talk about that man."

"Then you fancy that Meg is not interested in John?"

"Who?" cried Jo.

"Mr. Brooke. I call him 'John' now."

"Oh, dear! Now I know you'll take his part. He's been good to Father, and you will let Meg marry him!" And Jo pulled her hair again angrily.

"My dear, don't get angry. I will tell you how it happened. John was so devoted to Father that we couldn't help getting fond of him. He told us he loves Meg. But he wants to have a comfortable home before he asks her to marry him. Besides, Meg *is* young, and I need to see for myself what *her* feelings are for *him*."

"She'll see those handsome eyes, and then it will be all up with her," Jo grumbled. "She likes brown eyes, and doesn't think John an ugly name, and she'll go and fall in love, and there's an end of peace and fun, and cozy times together. I see it all! Brooke will carry her off, and make a hole in the family, and break my heart. Why weren't we all boys? Then there wouldn't be any bother." Jo leaned her chin on her knees sadly.

Mrs. March said, "Jo, it is natural you should all go to homes of your own in time. But I do want to keep my girls as long as I can. Your father and I have agreed that Meg shall not be engaged nor married before twenty. If she and John love one another, they can wait."

"Wouldn't you rather have her marry a rich man?" asked Jo.

"I *would* like John to be firmly established in some good business before they are married. But I also know how much genuine happiness can be found in a plain little house."

"Well, I hate to see things going all crisscross and getting snarled up," said Jo. "I wish we could keep from growing up. But buds turn into roses, and kittens into cats!"

"What's that about cats?" asked Meg. She crept into the room with a letter to Father in her hand.

"Only one of my stupid speeches. I'm going to bed," said Jo.

Mrs. March glanced over Meg's letter to Father. "It's beautifully written. Please add that I send my love to John," said Mrs. March as she gave it back.

"Do you call him *John*?" asked Meg, smiling.

"Yes. He has been like a son to us, and we are very fond of him," replied Mrs. March. She looked carefully at her daughter.

"I'm glad of that, for he is so lonely. Good-night, Mother," said Meg.

The kiss her mother gave her was very tender. As she went away, Mrs. March said, "She does not know if she loves John yet, but will soon."

CHAPTER EIGHTEEN

Father's Little Women

The peaceful weeks that followed were like sunshine after a storm.

Mr. March began to write of returning early in the new year. Beth was soon able to lie on the study sofa all day. She was able to play with her cats and dolls. Jo took her for a daily walk around the house. Meg cheerfully burned her white hands cooking. Amy celebrated her return by giving away many of her treasures.

Several days of mild weather led to a wonderful Christmas Day. Mr. March wrote that he would soon be with them. And Beth felt especially well that morning.

"I'm so full of happiness. If Father was here, that would be the last drop I could hold," said Beth.

"So am I," added Jo.

"I'm sure I am," echoed Amy.

"Of course I am!" cried Meg.

Now and then things do happen like in a storybook. Half an hour after everyone had said they were so happy they could only hold one drop more, the drop came. Laurie opened the parlor door and popped his head in very quietly.

He might as well have turned a somersault and whooped. His face was so full of excitement that everyone jumped up. He said, "Here's another Christmas present for the March family."

In Laurie's place stood Mr. March, leaning on Mr. Brooke. He tried to say something and couldn't. Of course there was a stampede. For several minutes everybody seemed to lose their wits.

Mr. March became lost in the embrace of four pairs of loving arms. Jo nearly fainted. Mr. Brooke kissed Meg—entirely by mistake, of course. Amy tumbled over a stool, and hugged and cried over her father's boots. Mrs. March was the first to recover herself. She said, "Hush! Remember Beth."

But it was too late. The study door flew open.
Beth ran straight into her father's arms. Then their
full hearts overflowed.

There never was such a Christmas dinner as the one they had that day—a plump turkey, plum pudding and all the fixings. Mr. Laurence and his grandson dined with them, as well as Mr. Brooke. Jo frowned at this, which amused Laurie.

Beth and her father sat in two easy chairs at the head of the table. They drank toasts, told stories, sang songs, and had a very good time.

After the guests left, the happy family sat together round the fire. Mr. March took little Beth in his lap, looked with pride on his girls, and said, "I have discovered many things today."

"Oh, tell us what they are!" cried Meg.

"Here is one." He picked up Meg's hand. "I remember when this hand was white and smooth and you wanted to keep it that way. It was very pretty then, but to me it is much prettier now. You have a hard palm and pricked fingers from much work. And in these scars and scratches I see a little history. Meg, my dear, I'm proud to shake this good, hard-working little hand."

"What about Jo? Please say something nice. She has tried so hard and been so very, very good to me," said Beth in her father's ear.

He laughed and looked across at the tall girl. "In spite of the new short hair, I don't see the 'son Jo' whom I left a year ago," said Mr. March. "I see a young lady. Her face is rather thin and pale, but I like to look at it. It is gentler. She moves quietly, and takes care of a certain little sister in a motherly way that delights me. I rather miss my wild girl. But if I get a strong, helpful, sweet woman in her place, I shall feel quite satisfied."

"Now it's Beth's turn," said Amy, longing for her turn, but ready to wait.

"There's so little of her, I'm afraid to say much, for fear she will slip away altogether. Though she is not so shy as she used to be," began their father cheerfully. But remembering how nearly he *had* lost her, he held her close. "I've got you safe, my Beth. And I'll keep you so, please God."

He looked down at Amy, who sat at his feet, and said, "I saw that Amy ran errands for her mother all afternoon. She has waited on everyone with patience and good humor. She does not complain much. And she has not even mentioned a very pretty ring that she wears. She has learned to think of other people more and of herself less."

Beth perked up and smiled broadly.

"What are you thinking of, Beth?" asked Jo.

"It's singing time now, and I want to be in my old place," Beth said softly. "I have put music to the poem Father likes. It is the 'Song of the Shepherd Boy.' "

So, sitting at the dear little piano, Beth softly touched the keys. And in the sweet voice they had never thought they would hear again, she sang a lovely hymn.

CHAPTER NINETEEN

The Year Closes

Mother and daughters hovered around Mr. March the next day as he sat propped up in a big chair by Beth's sofa. Their happiness seemed complete. But something seemed to be "in the air."

Mr. and Mrs. March looked at one another nervously. They watched Meg, who was absent-minded, shy, and silent. She jumped whenever the bell rang, and blushed when John Brooke's name was mentioned.

Laurie came by in the afternoon. Seeing Meg at the window, he fell down on one knee in the snow, beat his chest, tore at his hair, and clasped his hands together.

"What does the goose mean by that?" said Meg, laughing.

"He's showing you how your John will act," answered Jo miserably.

"Don't say *my John*. It isn't proper or true. Jo, I've told you I don't care much about him. There isn't to be anything said."

"But something *has* been said. I see it, and so does Mother. You are not like your old self a bit, and seem ever so far away from me. I do wish it was all settled. If you mean to do it, have it over quickly," said Jo.

"I can't say anything till he speaks. And he won't, because Father said I was too young," began Meg. She smiled in a way that suggested she did not quite agree with her father.

"If he *did* speak, what would you say?"

"I've planned it all. I will calmly say, 'Thank you, Mr. Brooke. You are very kind, but I agree with Father that I am too young.' "

A sudden step in the hall made Meg fly into her chair and begin to sew as if her life depended on it.

"Good afternoon, Miss Jo. I came to get my umbrella—I mean, to see how your father is today," said Mr. Brooke nervously.

"It's very well, thank you. He's in the umbrella stand. I'll get him, and tell the umbrella you are here." And having jumbled her father and the umbrella together, Jo left the room to give Meg a chance to make her speech. But the instant Jo vanished, Meg murmured, "Mother will like to see you. I'll call her."

"Don't go. Are you afraid of me, Margaret?" John asked. Meg blushed up to the little curls on her forehead, for he had only called her *Miss* Margaret before. Then she put out her hand and said, "How can I be afraid when you have been so kind to Father? I only wish I could thank you for it."

"Shall I tell you how?" asked Mr. Brooke, looking at Meg with so much love that her heart began to flutter. "I only want to know if you care for me a little, Meg. I love you so much."

This was the moment for her speech, but Meg forgot every word of it and answered, "I don't know."

He pressed her hand gratefully, and said, "Will you try and find out? I want to know so much."

Just at that moment, Aunt March came hobbling in. Mr. Brooke vanished into the study.

"Bless me, what's all this?" cried the old lady.

"It's Father's friend. I'm so surprised to see you!" stammered Meg.

"What is Father's friend saying to make you blush so?" returned Aunt March, sitting down.

"Mr. Brooke came for his umbrella," began Meg.

"Brooke? That boy's tutor? Ah! I understand now," cried Aunt March, looking shocked. "Do you mean to marry this man? If you do, not one penny of my money ever goes to you."

Now, if Aunt March had begged Meg to *accept* John Brooke, Meg probably would have declared she couldn't *think* of it. But when ordered *not* to like him, Meg immediately made up her mind that she would.

"I shall marry whom I please, Aunt March. You can leave your money to anyone you like!"

"Now, Meg, my dear, you ought to marry rich to help your family. I thought you had more sense."

"John is good and wise. He's got heaps of talent, he's willing to work, and he's so brave," said Meg.

"He knows you have rich relatives, child. That's why he likes you."

"Aunt March, how dare you say such a thing? My John wouldn't marry for money, any more than I would. I'm not afraid of being poor."

"Well, I wash my hands of the whole affair! Don't expect anything from me when you are married. I'm done with you forever."

Slamming the door in Meg's face, Aunt March left. Meg did not know whether to laugh or cry. Before she could make up her mind, she was embraced by Mr. Brooke.

"I couldn't help hearing, Meg. Thank you for defending me. You do care for me a little bit."

"I didn't know how much till Aunt March said those things about you," began Meg.

"May I stay and be happy, dear?"

"Yes, John," said Meg.

Fifteen minutes later, Jo came softly downstairs. At the door she saw something that stopped her. Her mouth was nearly as wide open as her eyes. There was Mr. Brooke, the enemy, sitting on the sofa with Meg upon his knee!

Jo gave a sort of gasp. Mr. Brooke laughed and said, "Sister Jo, congratulate us!"

Jo vanished without a word. She cried as she told the awful news to Beth and Amy. The little girls, however, thought it was a wonderful event, and Jo got little comfort from them.

Mr. and Mrs. March went into the parlor to talk with the happy couple. Mr. Brooke asked for Meg's hand in marriage, and they agreed to a wedding in three years, when Meg would be twenty.

Mr. Brooke proudly took Meg into supper that evening. They both looked so happy that Jo didn't have the heart to be jealous. No one ate much, but everyone looked very happy. The old room seemed to brighten up amazingly when the first romance of the family began there.

"You can't say nothing pleasant ever happens now, can you, Meg?" said Amy.

"No, I'm sure I can't. So much has happened since I said that!" answered Meg.

Mrs. March said, "This has been a year full of events, but it ends well, after all."

Old Mr. Laurence and his grandson came by. Laurie came prancing in bearing a great bridal-looking bouquet. He was invited to the wedding on the spot.

"I'll come if I'm at the ends of the earth, for the sight of Jo's face would alone be worth a long journey. Jo, what's the matter?" asked Laurie, following her into a corner of the parlor.

"You can't know how hard it is for me to give up Meg. I've lost my dearest friend."

"You've got me, anyhow. I'll stand by you all the days of my life." And Laurie meant what he said. "Don't be sad. Meg is happy. I shall be through college before long, and then we'll go to Europe on some nice trip."

"There's no knowing what may happen in three years," said Jo.

"That's true. Don't you wish you could see where we shall all be then? I do," returned Laurie.

Jo's eyes went slowly round the room, brightening as they looked. Father and Mother sat together, quietly reliving a romance which began some twenty years ago. Amy was drawing the lovebirds, who sat apart in a beautiful world of their own. Beth lay on her sofa, talking cheerily with old Mr. Laurence. Jo lounged in her favorite seat. Laurie, leaning on the back of her chair, smiled at her in the long mirror which reflected them both.

"I think not, for I might see something sad," said Jo. "Everyone looks so happy now. I don't believe they could be much improved."

And so the curtain falls—for now—upon Meg, Jo, Beth, and Amy in this first act of the story called *Little Women*.

The End of Part I — *Little Women*

Part II — *Good Wives*

ABOUT THE AUTHOR

LOUISA MAY ALCOTT

Louisa May Alcott was born in 1832 in Concord, Massachusetts. Her father was a brilliant thinker with famous writer friends, but he earned little money. In her teenage years, young Louisa helped to support her family. She was a schoolteacher and nurse, she took in sewing and laundry, and she worked as a maid. She also found time to write—stories, poems and plays—and published her first pieces when she was twenty-one.

For several years, Alcott supported her family by writing "thriller" or "romantic" stories. Then a publisher requested a book for girls, so Alcott wrote *Little Women*, using her own life with her four sisters as inspiration. (She put herself in the story—as Jo March.) The book was published in 1868. It became an immediate success, and remains a favorite classic to this day. Part Two was published in 1869 as *Good Wives*, and the two parts were reissued as a single book in 1871.

Alcott wrote several more books about the March family, including *Little Men* (1871), and *Jo's Boys* (1886). She also worked for women's rights. Alcott died in Boston in 1888.